Escape

IN STYLE

Escape

IN STYLE

To the World's Most Enchanting Homes and Villas

By Robert Schoolsky

Created by Edmund Gudenas

Park Street Press

ROCHESTER · VERMONT

Park Street Press
One Park Street
Rochester, Vermont 05767

Library of Congress Cataloging-in-Publication Data

Schoolsky, Robert.
  Escape in style to the world's most enchanting
homes and villas.

  1. Vacation homes. I. Gudenas, Edmund. II. Title.
HD7289.2.S36   1988   643'.2   88-17832
ISBN 0-89281-240-0

Design by Ann Aspell
Part opening calligraphy by Rene Schall.

Title page Photograph: *Magic Lady*

Printed and bound in Italy
10 9 8 7 6 5 4 3 2 1

Park Street Press is a division of Inner Traditions International, Ltd.

Distributed to the book trade in the United States by Harper and Row Publishers, Inc.

Distributed to the book trade in Canada by Book Center, Inc., Montreal, Quebec

Contents

CASTLES AND COURTS

ESCAPE WITHOUT BOUNDS

Foreword

Escape in Style has been created with one goal in mind—to open up a world of enchantment that we often hear about but rarely have the opportunity to enter into personally. More than twenty dazzling homes are featured here with narrative that traces their history from medieval times to the present, bringing life to mortar and stone. Once available only as fiction or fantasy, today each of these luxurious residences stands ready to provide you with the vacation of a lifetime.

Although it is not intended to be another travel guide or book on interior decoration, the exceptional photography and descriptive material contained in *Escape* would qualify it for either category. You will be able, based on the material provided, to visualize the homes in detail, to sense their ambiance, and to feel yourself a part of a unique and alluring milieu.

The owners have not paid to have their homes included. Rather, our editor has chosen from a number of contenders the most extraordinary residences available for rent or lease. If you own or represent a special home that you would like us to consider for a future publication, or if you have any comments on this one, please return the bound reply card attached to this volume or write to me:

Edmund Gudenas
Escape in Style
Park Street Press
One Park Street
Rochester, Vermont 05767

Please be advised that our "particulars" data is based upon information supplied by the agency or individual listed with each property and is in effect at the time of printing. The owners or agents take full responsibility for all arrangements and details regarding your visit.

I would like to thank Robert D. Gries, Richard F. Brezic, and Tom Czernicki for their invaluable assistance on this project.

Edmund Gudenas

Introduction

In Xanadu did Kubla Khan
A stately pleasure dome decree:
Where Alph, the sacred river, ran
Through caverns measureless to man
Down to a sunless sea.
So twice five miles of fertile ground
With walls and towers were girdled round.

Samuel Taylor Coleridge

In the latter half of the 20th century one need not travel to Xanadu seeking a pleasure dome. Magnificent residences are accessible on every continent, touching every sea, and sometimes even hidden away in our own backyards, providing temporary escape from the cares of the world.

From the outset, I was intrigued with the idea of writing a book on the world's most luxurious homes for lease or rent. My work as a wine, food, and travel writer has taken me throughout the world seeking the unusual. Even so, I was unprepared for the broad scope of material gathered for *Escape in Style.*

Ed Gudenas, who conceived this project almost four years ago, presented the concept of a grand "coffee table book" of the world's most desirable residences available for as little as a week or as long as a year. Through his meticulous research, the very best material extant on this theme was made available. The difficult job of selecting the most desirable homes was carried out by my editor, Estella Arias, whose good taste, sense of style, and instinct for detail are evident on every page.

Escape in Style is intended to be much more than an armchair journey into the dream realm of a privileged few. We offer it as an invitation to experience this domain firsthand on your next vacation or sabbatical. The halcyon retreat or the romantic weekend you've long envisioned are actually achievable in any of these homes, or you can bring a group of friends together for an un-forgettable celebration.

Our detailed descriptions of the homes include an exploration of their rich history, design, and architecture, as well as infor-mation on regional food and wine, sporting opportunities, cultural events, and exclusive entertainment spots. These details may serve as a springboard to further investigation of your contemplated destination. Names and addresses of owners or agents are given along with highlights of the services available with each home.

Many of the residences are located in a sportsman's paradise, with tennis, golf, and horseback riding on the grounds. Alterna-tively, the staff can arrange guest facilities for these sports at nearby locations if advised of your requirements in advance.

It is our hope that the world of elegance, enjoyment, luxury, and beauty contained in these pages will help you plan-and realize-the perfect escape.

Robert Schoolsky

Homes without Equal

The Great House

*I*ts white domes shimmer in the tropical sun, framed by the azure waters of the Caribbean and the emerald green fronds of its cordon of royal palms. At a glance, it summons up images of the most glorious palaces of the Orient, reconstructed in a magical domain. It is Great House, home of Lord Glenconner (né Colin Tennant), owner and developer of the island of Mustique.

Situated on twenty-three acres of valley flatland, adjoining 450 feet of one of the island's most exquisite beaches, Great House has often been described as a mini Taj Mahal. Its main building opens onto a stunning seventy-foot-long marble reflecting/swimming pool. Three guest cottages, with thatched roofs in a traditional Thai design, accent Great House as a superb place for the enjoyment of convivial hospitality.

Central to the design and spirit of Great House was Lord Glenconner's emphatic desire to avoid anything "cute or colonial" in his island residence. The result was a collection of sumptuous architectural styles informed by a lively sense of humor, combining elements from nearly every part of what was once the English empire's farthest reaches. In its furnishings, too, Great House plays upon Asia's fascination with mother-of-pearl, ebony, china, and glass. Yet there is a method to this house's particular madness. Every item of furniture in Great House has been chosen or fashioned to withstand the island's sea air.

Construction of Great House started in the mid-seventies, after Lord Glenconner's personal survey (some of it "on location") of materials and themes from India, Turkey, and China, not to mention Indonesia, Hong Kong, and the Phillipines. A magnificent outdoor pavilion in the form of an Indian temple, for instance, was shipped to Mustique from Delhi in 180 crates. Dating from

Previous page: *The living room is defined by four thirteen-foot-high concrete columns, topped by copper palm fronds at the capitals.* Right: *The outdoor pavilion, in the form of an Indian temple, was shipped to Mustique from Delhi in 180 crates and reconstructed over a three-month period. Dating from the late eighteenth century, the pavilion is remarkable for its white marble latticework.*

the late eighteenth century, the pavilion is remarkable for its white marble latticework. Lord Glenconner himself supervised its painstaking reconstruction over a three-month period.

Great House's main villa is an eclectic blend of motifs that include Thai latticework on windows and archways with a central dome patterned after the Hagia Sophia in Istanbul. The dome itself is finished in Chinese tiles and native coral blocks transported from Barbados; other building materials used abundantly include teak, copper, and marble. The villa has a total of eleven rooms, including a palatial and glamorous twenty-four-foot-square living room flanked with sitting rooms. Defined by four thirteen-feet-high concrete columns fashioned to appear as palm trees (topped by copper palm fronds at the capitals), the room has a distinctly Edwardian-era feeling, reminiscent of the glories of the British Raj.

The music room of Great House, which features a coquina marble floor, provides access to the master bedroom. Twin peacocks frame the ornate silver bed in the master bedroom, which features an ample dressing room and is fully air-conditioned. Lavish travertine baths adjoin both guest bedrooms. Situated near the garden, Great House's sleeping accommodations offer guests an opportunity to dream in unparalleled luxury.

Every item of furniture in Great House has been chosen or fashioned to withstand the island's sea air.

Below: *A broad expanse of white beach is the only barrier between the Great House and the inviting waters of the Caribbean.* Right: *In its furnishings, Great House plays upon Asia's fascination with mother-of-pearl, ebony, china, and glass.* Next page: *Twin peacocks frame the ornate silver bed in the master bedroom.*

Great House is the result of a professional collaboration between Arne Hasselquist and the late world-famous set designer Oliver Messel, who together were responsible for most of its unique structural designs. The villa now stands as the pinnacle of their joint accomplishments and the most distinctive and luxurious residence in Mustique, if not the Caribbean.

Mustique itself is a highly romantic setting. A dependency of Saint Vincent, the island is located at a point 110 miles from Barbados and 60 miles from Saint Lucia. Lord Glenconner became acquainted with the island in 1959 while still known as Colin Tennant, purchased it, and received a royal charter created by an act of Parliament to form the ruling home-owners' association.

While part of the enchantment of Great House derives from its placement on a charmed isle in the midst of the Caribbean, the greater part derives from the imagination with which it was built. How many other houses in the Western world embody such regal architectural boldness with so much lighthearted grace?

PARTICULARS

Details:
Three Thai-style guest cottages on the grounds with private suites
Two-bedroom staff cottage
Two two-bedroom suites in the Great House with two additional staff bedrooms
Garage on premises

Contact:
The Mustique Co. Ltd.
P.O. Box 349
St. Vincent and the Grenadines
West Indies

Telephone:
(809) 458-4621/4653

Situated on twenty-three acres of valley flatland adjoining 450 feet of one of the island's most exquisite beaches, Great House has often been described as a mini Taj Mahal.

Villa
La Loggia

A verdant plain sweeps down from the peaks of the Dolomite Mountains to Venice, "queen of the Adriatic," Italy's ancient gateway to the Orient. This is Venetia, the region of timeless beauty known to Italians as the Veneto. Over the centuries it has attracted countless poets and artists who sought to inspire their muse, including Shakespeare (who set *Romeo and Juliet* in Verona and the story of Shylock in Venice), Lord Byron, and Thomas Mann.

At the very heart of the region, in the province of Treviso, is Villa La Loggia. Built in 1610 on the remains of an ancient fortress, it perches high on a hill in a dominant position that once provided a strategic command of the countryside and today offers its visitors far-reaching, idyllic views. Its oasislike beauty and serenity—a startling contrast to the hectic pace of Italy's urban cities—has drawn such noted guests as Lord Snowdon, Queen Ellen of Romania, members of the Italian royal family, and (most recently) Paloma Picasso.

Still in the possession of the descendants of its original owners, Villa La Loggia offers visitors the opportunity to enjoy gracious Venetian living in a setting that is strongly influenced by the Byzantine and Gothic architecture of nearby Venice. Resident guests can delight in the grand salons and gardens that hearken back to a time far removed from the twentieth century, yet without forfeiting any modern conveniences. High ceilings with carved beams sweep over immaculate tiled floors, and original artwork decorates most rooms, while the splendid seventeenth-century frescoes and richly ornate Venetian furnishings are artfully counterbalanced by such elements as the swimming pool, telephones and television, modern bathrooms, and up-to-date kitchen.

The villa's multilevel design provides four bedrooms, each

with a unique vista, containing a total of nine beds. Three living rooms, a salon, and a dining room afford sufficient space for entertaining on a grand scale. The spacious courtyard and main entrance form the gateway to a monumental staircase leading up to a frescoed living room and a bedroom with double bed and bathroom. One flight up is the top floor with its grand dining room and main salon. An extensive veranda leads to the garden and pool. Outdoor dining can be arranged on the veranda.

The first of three lower levels contains a living room with a magnificent fireplace and two bedrooms, one with two beds and bath, the other with a single bed and bath. The second sublevel features another living room and a bedroom with two single beds and bath. The lowest level houses the kitchen and dining area; a dumbwaiter leads to the main dining room five flights above.

Just two kilometers from La Loggia is a charming inn where additional guests may be housed. Tennis courts are available at the nearby town of Solighetto, and a golf course is located in Cansiglio, thirty kilometers from the villa. Villa Loggia is available during the prime season (May through August).

Natives of the Veneto are friendly, outgoing people, descendants of the hardy mariners and crafty traders who made the Rialto the marketplace of the world. They are justly proud of their home, for Venetia offers nourishment at every level to native residents and visitors alike. Whether one dines at the villa, in a cozy *trattoria* or a grand *restaurante,* a superb regional cuisine can be savored ranging from basic *polenta* or rice and beans to a classical *risotto* with fresh game or fish. Here the palate can be tantalized with fresh catches from the Adriatic and prime-quality wine from the region's stores. To nourish the mind, the region offers a vast wealth of culture and art, as mirrored in the dramatic beauty of its cities. And finally, one's inner being can be refreshed by walks through the Venetian landscape, with its lush fields of wheat, rice, corn, and olives.

Previous page: *Villa La Loggia's three living rooms, with original art and frescoes, are strongly influenced by the Byzantine and Gothic architecture of nearby Venice.*
Right: *The dining room and its ornate, seventeenth century Venetian furnishings provide the ideal setting for enjoying superb regional cuisine.*

Above: *Built in 1610 on the remains of an ancient fortress, Villa La Loggia perches high on a hill with idyllic views of the countryside.* Right: *In another living room, high ceilings, carved beams, and tile floors blend tastefully with the art and furnishings.*

PARTICULARS

Details:
Four bedrooms
Accommodates nine
Two maids, cook
gardener

Contact:
The Best in Italy
via Ugo Foscolo, 72
Florence, Italy

Telephone:
055-223064

Cedar Grove Mansion

Deep in the American heartland, paddleboats with their ghostly white painted surfaces still ply the waters of the Mississippi, making stops along the river for tourists and cargo wending their way down to New Orleans. The river towns evoke images of the world of Twain and Faulkner, a region firmly linked to the nation's past. This was the western flank of the Old South, a land of stately mansions and sprawling plantations. Cedar Grove, a mansion residence in Vicksburg, Mississippi, still exists as a gateway to that antebellum world.

The construction of Cedar Grove—a wedding present built by John A. Klein for his bride—began in 1840 and was completed less than a decade before the outbreak of the war between the states. The Kleins' European honeymoon inspired them over the following years to incorporate many architectural amenities into their new home.

Today, Cedar Grove is one of the South's largest and loveliest historic mansions. Miraculously, the house survived the ravages of the battle of Vicksburg, although a Union cannonball still remains lodged in a parlor wall. The ball was left in place by Mrs. Klein, a niece of General Sherman, who used it as evidence to assure her neighbors that she had not been given special consideration by her uncle's troops during the Union assault.

Vicksburg was the last southern stronghold, the "Gibraltar of the Confederacy." The fall of the city, following a spectacular forty-seven-day siege, was the turning point of the war. Now history and military buffs flock to Vicksburg each year to visit the National Military Park and Cemetery, one of the best-marked battlefield areas in the country. The whole length of fortifications and the trenches of the besiegers can be followed along Confederate and Union Avenues, and an overview of the final siege can be gained by a visit to the museum in the National Park headquarters.

Cedar Grove, itself a living museum, contains one of the South's largest and finest collections of furnishings from the antebellum period. Gaslight chandeliers cast their flickering shadows against gold leaf mirrors and Italian marble mantels. Pink, cream, and white walls and ceilings in the main rooms are embellished with carved moldings and ornamental plaster carvings. Full-length drapes frame the towering windows, and everywhere the original wooden furniture gleams.

Previous page: *On a four-acre estate, Cedar Grove Mansion stands amidst sculptured gardens, gazebos, and fountains.* Below: *The landscaped grounds reveal many touches of European influence, inspired by the Klein's honeymoon journey.* Right: *Cedar Grove contains one of the South's largest and finest collections of furnishings from the antebellum period.*

PARTICULARS

Details:
Accommodates thirty-six
Fully staffed
Dining and banquet facilities
Eighteen bedrooms
Swimming pool, formal gardens, spa

Contact:
Cedar Grove Mansion
2200 Oak Street
Vicksburg, Mississippi
39180

Telephone:
(800) 862-1300
(601) 636-1605

Three separate residences are available to guests. The guest house features two bedrooms and a swimming pool set in a brick courtyard. Flanking the mansion on the opposite side is the carriage house, which contains eight suites, some with fireplaces. The mansion itself contains a master suite and eight double bedrooms. All suites and bedrooms have private baths.

The public rooms are varied and sumptuous. Jefferson Davis once danced in the magnificent ballroom and no doubt retired during the evening's festivities to the stately library for port, cigars, and a discussion of politics. Three parlors and a huge dining room are also available for tasting a world now "gone with the wind."

Far left: *The master bedroom is named after the Union General Grant who directed the siege of Vicksburg, establishing his reputation as a military genius.* Left: *Cedar Grove's formal dining room.*

Schloss Schlatt

Deep in Central Europe, bordered on the west by the Rhine basin and the Black Forest, to the south by the Swabian-Jura Alps, and to the east by the Harz mountain range is the Baden-Württemburg region of West Germany. Where warring tribes of Goths and Franks once held sway and Roman legions ruled, ancient towns and quaint villages pose against a landscape better suited to the world of Hansel and Gretel than to the twentieth century. It is the perfect setting for Schloss Schlatt, a sixteenth-century "kleines Landschloss"—a little Renaissance country palace. A short drive from Zurich-Klothen Airport, in a tiny village just over the Swiss border, this southern German retreat is convenient to all of Europe's major economic centers.

Although the interior of the building has been partly renovated to bring its furnishings up to the modern-day standards of its present owner, Count Patrick Douglas, the outer facade is as charming as when it was first built in 1580 to serve as the residence of the baron of Reischach.

The addition of a full-size swimming pool, several modern bathrooms, and a modern kitchen complement and balance the large bedrooms and main entertaining rooms, which are furnished with original seventeenth- and eighteenth-century furniture.

Set in a formal garden and surrounded by a well-maintained private glade, the castle provides privacy yet is just outside the local village. Ten minutes away by automobile is Lake Constance, the longest lake in Europe (fifty miles) and one of the loveliest. A motorboat maintained at the lake by Count Douglas is at the disposal of guests for waterskiing and sightseeing.

The vast estate of the Douglas family—over fifteen thousand acres of hunting grounds—is open to guests for horseback riding (horses are available from a nearby academy) and some of the best red deer hunting in all of Europe.

The Douglas family owns the 15,000 acres of forest land surrounding their country palace, ideal for biking, horseback riding, deer hunting, or long leisurely walks.

37

Above: *Schloss Schlatt was built in 1580 as the local residence for the baron of Reischach, landlord of most of the forest and farming land in the area. Today, it is owned by Count Patrick Douglas* who uses it as a countryside home. Right: *A timelessness is created by the cozy stove and other seventeenth- and eighteenth-century pieces found throughout this little palace in the country.*

PARTICULARS

Details:
Eight rooms with double beds
Accommodates a maximum of seventeen guests
Two kitchens
Residence caretaker and wife
English-speaking cook available
Mercedes-Benz 230E car available
Three tennis courts within walking distance

Contact:
Count Patrick Douglas or Mrs. Therese Van Loo
Gloriettegasse 6
Vienna, Austria

Telephone:
(Vienna) 0222-604 45 70
(U.S.) (301) 986-8830
       Mrs. Gisela Ormsby

James II House

*F*or centuries the rolling fields and market towns of western England have been a haven for the prosperous mercantile families of Britain, who erected their "stately homes in miniature" amid the quintessential British landscape of woodland, moor, valley, and mountain. Nestled among picturebook Cotswold villages with such lyrical names as Stow-on-the-Wold, yet only one and a half hours from London by train, is the James II House, described by English architectural connoisseurs as one of the finest small houses in the country.

Built in 1688, two hundred years after the reign of its namesake (who is remembered for regulating the nation's coinage), the residence retains most of its original features and yet is invitingly comfortable. The house is beautifully decorated throughout, reflecting the care and taste that have been maintained by continuing family ownership. Highlights are a fine collection of contemporary and antique furniture and paintings, a magnificent seventeenth-century Belgian tapestry, and an impressive display of the needlework of seven generations of the owning family.

A warm entry hall beckons visitors into the richly paneled drawing room, with its deep sofas and huge open log fireplace under an ornately carved mantelpiece. The main rooms on the ground floor include a library-study adorned with pieces of rare sculpture and an attractive dining room with its own fireplace and porcelain objets d'art. The kitchen and a utility room complete the lower floor.

Upstairs (the first floor, in British terminology) is the master suite, dominated by a canopy-crowned double bed, connecting bathroom, and two twin-bedded rooms, each with a connecting bathroom and separate dressing room with cloakroom/W.C.

The second floor contains two single bedrooms, a snug sitting

Nestled among Cotswold villages is the James II House, described by English architectural connoisseurs as one of the finest small houses in the country.

room, an additional bedroom with two single beds, and a Laura Ashley bathroom.

The house is set on five acres of grounds; two acres form a formal garden in the rear, which in turn opens onto pastures with far-reaching views of the surrounding Cotswold countryside. A variety of fresh fruits and vegetables are grown in the kitchen garden to complement the cornucopia of seasonal produce from the surrounding farms and market towns. A Cordon Bleu cook is available on request to plan and execute menus befitting the dining table of this stately manor.

The dense woods of the countryside are relieved by pasture-lands abundant with grazing flocks of sheep, and there are outstanding opportunities for long walks and motorcar exploration. Cirencester, England's largest wool market from the thirteenth to

Below: The bright, attractive master suite is dominated by a canopy-crowned double bed, set in the atmosphere of a comfortable sitting room.

Right: *An example of the family's fine needlework skills.* Next page: *The richly paneled drawing room has a magnificent seventeenth-century Belgian tapestry, antique paintings, and a huge open log-fireplace.*

the fifteenth century, contains an excellent museum with treasured material from the Roman period, when the ancient city was the juncture of five important roads.

Other areas of historic interest in the region include Bath and its restored Roman ruins, Warwick Castle, Stoneleigh Abbey, and Coventry, Oxford, Blenheim Place (the ancestral home of the Dukes of Marlborough and birthplace of Sir Winston Churchill), and Stratford-upon-Avon.

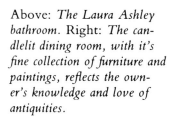

Above: *The Laura Ashley bathroom.* Right: *The candlelit dining room, with it's fine collection of furniture and paintings, reflects the owner's knowledge and love of antiquities.*

PARTICULARS

Details:
Accommodates eight
Staff of two
Daily maid service

Contact:
Blandings
V. G. Williams Inc.
International Properties
2841 29th Street NW
Washington, D.C. 20008

Telephone:
(Vienna) 0222–604 45 70
(U.S.) (301) 986–8830
Mrs. Gisela Ormsby

Farley House

*F*ew regions of the United States have played such a key role in the development of the nation as the state of Virginia. From the founding of the first English settlement at Jamestown through the turbulent prerevolutionary period and the planning of independence, it furnished the embryonic world power with some of its greatest presidents and statesmen. A leader in the movement that led to the Revolution and the chief battleground of the Civil War, Virginia saw the introduction of slavery and the last confrontation between the states, and furnished part of the land for the establishment of the District of Columbia.

A silent witness to this panoramic passage of history is Farley House, an imposing Federal-style mansion in Virginia's Piedmont region. A handsome plantation dwelling almost two hundred years old, Farley House—along with such celebrated mansions as Belmont, Oatlands, Carter Hall, and Annefield—set the style of grandeur in the Old South. Set against the backdrop of the Blue Ridge Mountains, the mansion sits on a property of 103 acres, divided into 8 acres of landscaped lawn, 35 acres of fenced pasture, and 60 acres of mature woods.

Simplicity, craftsmanship, and dignified refinement are the hallmarks of Farley's construction. Hand woodwork is found throughout the house, with all of the furniture carefully selected to reflect the Federal period decor. Recent preservation and restoration efforts have returned Farley to its original design. Today, it offers guests a distinctive and luxurious retreat.

The outer facade is magnificent, with nine bay windows on each of the first and second floors framed by black shutters. Twin

Previous page: *Farley House is one of the few remaining structures in Culpepper County to be placed on both the register of Virginia Landmarks Commission and the National Register of Historic Places.* Above: *Farley's dining room.*

north and south galleries run along the entire length of the house, providing access to the library, living room, dining room, and kitchen. Twin staircases lead to the bedrooms on the second floor, which are connected by a central gallery.

Farley is one of the few remaining properties in Culpepper County of such architectural, military, and social significance that it has been placed on both the register of the Virginia Landmarks Commission and the National Register of Historic Places. In 1863 it served as headquarters for Union General John Sedgwick during the Battle of Brandy Station, the largest cavalry campaign of the Civil War. It was on the steps of Farley that General Sedgwick was photographed by the great Civil War photographer, Matthew Brady.

Today the scene is one of complete tranquility with a rural atmosphere of green lawns, pasture land, and acres of dense woods. Outside of Culpepper County is Commonwealth Park, one of Virginia's largest and most active equestrian centers. Nearby Brandy Station is a quaint country town. Fine restaurants, shopping, and sports facilities are all a short distance from the residence.

Below: *Hand woodwork is found throughout the house, with all of the furniture carefully selected to reflect the Federal period decor.*

PARTICULARS

Details:
Ten-room residence with four bedrooms
Three bathrooms (one with Jacuzzi)
Heated swimming pool
Completely modernized kitchen with all appliances
Separate complete apart-ment in basement of east wing
Guest house on premises with kitchenette, bath and living area
Daily maid service

Contact:
Blandings
V. G. Williams Inc.
International Properties
2841 29th Street NW
Washington, D.C. 20008

Telephone:
(202) 328-1353

Right: *Many of the volumes in this magnificent library contain material that bears witness to Farley's history and origins.*

Take to the Waters

Villa Nuvolari

R ome may be the "eternal city," but southern Italy, particularly the area below Naples, is firmly linked with antiquity. Even after centuries of influence and domination by Normans, Spaniards, and marauders from Africa, the Mezzogiorano ("land of the midday sun") remains literally unchanged since the era when nearby Pompeii served as a playground for the nobility of imperial Rome.

It is more than a timelessness that pervades the atmosphere along the famous Amalfi Drive from Sorrento to the sweeping Bay of Salerno. Here, in the heart of Italy's Southern Riviera, amid a wild rustic beauty, palatial villas cling to seaside cliffs. The air is scented by lemon trees planted precariously in terrace groves. Here is Villa Nuvolari, one of the best-known works of modern architectural design on a coast already famous for its splendid properties.

The villa is actually built into the rugged mountainside. Hence there are no immediate neighbors to interfere or disturb Villa Nuvolari's sense of privacy or mar its many terraces' spectacular views of the sea and the town of Positano, an international resort on the Tyrrhenian Sea.

Villa Nuvolari, only twenty years old, was a unique concept born from the encounter between the architect Alfredo Freda and the poet Luciano Nuvolari. Their intention was to give a modern interpretation to the thousand-year-old architectural examples found along the Amalfi coast. Scholars consider the prevailing regional style to be one of three "natural" schools of design in the architectural world (the other two being Japanese and Tirolese).

Retaining antiquarian curves and lines, Freda and Nuvolari gave their creation considerable inner space, reworking and softening the familiar use of arches and angles. All ninety-degree angles

Previous page: *Built into the rugged mountainside, Villa Nuvolari offers spectacular views of the sea and the town of Positano.* Above: *An example of careful design by architect Alfredo Freda and poet Luciano Nuvolari, the longer lengths of all rooms face the sea to capture onshore breezes.* Right: *Delicate tile work and the softening of arches and angles are evidence of ancient Egyptian, Greek, Roman, and Moorish influence.*

were abolished in the scheme, replaced by the rounded curves that are the Villa's dominating decorative theme. Instead of traditional regional stone, the villa's thick outer walls were crafted from volcanic rock, which is highly resistant to temperature changes. Even on the hottest days in summer the house is cool.

All the rooms are rectangular, with the longer lengths always facing the sea. The interior design of the bedrooms, bathrooms, and floors are the exquisite work of local artisans who still endow their creations with the expertise of a bygone era. Furnishings were inspired by the refined and simple idea that "there is always a place for a thing of beauty and good taste."

The villa's location makes it an ideal central point from which to visit some of the world's most romantic destinations. Naples, with its teeming bay, and Blue Grotto are close by; the ruins of Pompeii are within excursion distance. Positano is surrounded by such internationally renowned resorts as Capri, Sorrento, Palinuro, Amalfi, and the beautiful Isle of Ischia.

PARTICULARS

Details:
The villa is comprised of two apartments that may be taken as one or separately.

Combined total of eight bedrooms accommodating thirteen guests

Fully equipped modern kitchens in both apartments

Gardener's cottage also available (bedroom, living room, eat-in kitchen)

Small children's swimming pool

The services of a cook and maid can be arranged

Contact:
Sharon J. Handler, Esq.
Rubin & Bailin
575 Madison Avenue
New York, N.Y. 10022

Telephone:
(212) 688-1210

Clinging to the rugged mountainside, the villa affords a sweeping view of Italy's Southern Riviera, unchanged since the days of imperial Rome.

Villa Playita

*I*t is a land of rugged beauty bordered by arid deserts, tropical jungles, volcanic mountain ranges, and the awesome splendor of a majestic ocean. It is a timeless land bearing the remnants of six thousand years of history in the form of ancient temples, ruins of once great cities, fortresslike palaces, and humble villages.

This is Mexico, home of the great Mayan and Aztec civilizations, a magnet for the Spanish conquistadors who came to conquer and rule. Their presence and power were fleeting moments in time, but each enriched the country's heritage of art and design with elements that are still present in today's foremost contemporary Mexican architecture.

Villa Playita is located at the heart of the Mexican Riviera, the golden strip of dazzling sand that traces the curve of the Pacific on Mexico's western coast. Although only a short drive from Manzanillo Airport, this fable-like architectural gem sits proudly above the ocean at the tip of the Santiago Peninsula. It was built (and is still owned today) by television personality Lyle Waggoner and his wife, Sharon, who use it as a private retreat.

The Villa is behind the guarded porticos of the Las Hadas community and is hidden from view by the surrounding Pacific seacoast jungle. Entering its graceful arched stone gateway is like stepping into a time warp, far from the twentieth century. Here, privacy is the keyword and elegance a way of life. Guests of the Waggoners over the years have included actors John Forsythe and Cliff Robertson.

Villa Playita is an "al fresco" delight, artfully designed to take advantage of the gentle ocean breezes which create year-round soothing temperatures. A roof handwoven from palm fronds soars forty-five feet above the interior living area, whose décor is complemented by furnishings in *manta*, Indian handwoven fabrics. The

Waggoners went deep into the jungle on horseback to personally pick out the huge palm fronds.

While all of the rooms are spacious, the living room, with walls washed in true Aztec colors and a tiled floor accented in Aztec design, is particularly stunning. The dining area table and floor are made of matching Mexican "rose" marble. Guests can literally swim up to the bar in the rock-formed pool, whose waters flow out to the patio and there cascade over the edge of the cliff.

The guest bedrooms all have private baths and patios with ocean views, but each has unique individually designed features. The master bedroom has an indoor pool and a sitting room with a carved peacock-shaped bed. The master bath overlooks banana and papaya groves. The aptly named Shell Guest Room is dominated by a coquille-shaped bed crowned by a cloud of white netting.

Left: Guests can swim up to the bar in the rock-formed pool, whose waters flow out to the patio and there cascade over the edge of the cliff. Above: The spacious living room, with walls washed in true Aztec colors and tiled floors with Aztec design.

Two tennis courts, reserved for the exclusive use of a few private villas, are a short stroll away. Waterskiing, wind surfing, and deep-sea fishing are available at the Hotel Las Hadas, as are night snorkeling, a particularly fascinating activity, and a Pete and Roy Dye–designed championship golf course. For those who wish to explore further, the great cosmopolitan resort city of Acapulco lies to the south.

PARTICULARS

Details:
A housekeeper/cook and waiter/chauffeur are included

Contact:
Sharon Waggoner
4450 Balboa Avenue
Encino, CA 91316

Telephone:
(818) 995-7332

Left: *A roof handwoven from palm fronds soars forty-five feet above the interior living area.* Far left: *The shell guest room, with its coquille-shaped bed crowned in a cloud of white netting, has its own living room.*

Villa Nirvana

*I*t is day's end in Acapulco. The arc of the bay, vividly framed against a copper-gold sky, is accented by thousands of twinkling lights that ring the shore. High on the eastern side of the bay, four Roman columns suddenly turn to flaming beacons in a nightly salute to the setting sun. Twilight has come to Villa Nirvana.

The nightly ritual of illumination is only one of the unusual features of a residence that *Town and Country* has called the most beautiful and elegant villa in Acapulco. This grand salon in a world-famous Edenesque setting has been featured in articles in *Vogue, House Beautiful, The New York Times,* and *Der Stern.* Located in the heights of Las Brisas, an exclusive residential section, it is Acapulco's most luxurious private domicile.

The international roster of guests who have stayed at Nirvana over the years attests to the universality of its appeal: Henry Ford II, Hugh Hefner, Shirley MacLaine, the Shah of Iran, Richard Burton, and Henry Kissinger are just a few of the names we can mention. The reason for their choice is clear. Villa Nirvana is a home of timeless beauty, aeons away from the plastic-and-chrome era that flourishes at some of the world's leading resorts and hotels. Nor has any expense been spared in cultivating this beauty. Attention has been given to every detail, from the hand-inlaid backgammon set in the game room to the fully-equipped modern kitchen, where a chef expertly prepares outstanding menus that feature local specialties.

On arrival at Nirvana—a Sanskrit name meaning "the region of highest bliss"—one is immediately transported to a milieu of near-mystical beauty. The entrance leads through an elaborate wrought-iron latticework gate that guards a pure white marble inner courtyard. It is a very private realm, created by the builder

Vividly framed against a copper-gold sky, four Roman columns turn to flaming beacons in a nightly salute to the setting sun.

69

Located in the heights of Las Brisas, an exclusive residential section, Villa Nirvana is Acapulco's most luxurious private domicile.

Oscar Obregon to permit entertaining on a lavish scale. Its various levels of chambers, terraces, pools, and bathrooms afford spectacular views of the resort area and the bay.

The main level is dominated by formal living and dining rooms decorated in Louis XVI style. The majestic "White House" terrace, also on the main level, leads out to a semicircular pool and a magnificent sundeck and garden which overlook the entire bay and open sea. A lower level features the Honeymoon Suite, a full-length terrace, and an outsize pool which extends into the bedroom. Each of the eight Roman-style baths (one for each bedroom) is finished in marble or onyx tile.

Acapulco, dramatically situated on the Pacific Ocean only 150 miles west of Mexico City, is one of the world's most exotic playgrounds. Its crystal-blue bay and white sand beaches combine

On arrival at Nirvana—a Sanskrit name meaning "the region of highest bliss"—one is immediately transported to a milieu of near-mystical beauty. One of the two entrances leads through an elaborate wrought-iron latticework gate.

with exciting nightclubs and elegant restaurants to create Mexico's best-known resort area. The region boasts a long and colorful history with traditional ties to the Orient. Yet the city itself is quite new. Countless hotels, starting from the water's edge, cover the hillside and extend to the mountains beyond, creating a wonderland atmosphere of facilities designed to please the most jaded taste. Nor does consideration of season need to enter anyone's vacation plans here, for the climate is virtually perfect year-round. Days are filled with such challenges as deep-sea fishing and para-sailing, as well as such traditional activities as golf, tennis, horse-back riding, and shopping at the area's international boutiques. Evenings are romantic, with dining and dancing under ink-blue, star-filled skies.

PARTICULARS

Details:
Eight double bedrooms
Ten bathrooms
Two swimming pools
Two kitchens
Residence staff of four plus
international cook
Completely air-conditioned
Guest membership at the
exclusive Club La Concha
can be arranged.
Golf and tennis available at
nearby Princess Hotel

Contact:
Oscar Obregon
Avenida: Melchor Ocampo
344
Mexico City, Mexico
06500

Telephone:
5117181–51479091

Previous page: *A wide view
of the unique honeymoon
suite on the lower level. A
balustrade terrace runs the
length of the suite alongside
the pool which extends into
the bedroom.* Left: *The aptly
named "White House" terrace
leads out to the semicircular
pool and a magnificent sundeck and garden that overlook
the entire bay and open sea.*

Escape to the Islands

Casa
dalla Valle

Ranking among the most comfortable homes on Mustique is Casa Dalla Valle, a six-bedroom villa of Spanish Mediterranean design that has been renovated in a novel style that captures the full flavor of the island and its natural elements.

Perched on ten hillside acres, Casa Dalla Valle offers its guests a surfeit of amenities for both indoor and outdoor living, with a large sundeck, a patio, and both a covered terrace and poolside terrace adjoining its outdoor dining gazebo. Stepped gardens fan outward and downward from the villa toward the beach directly below the house. Because of its magnificent coastal setting, too, Casa Dalla Valle affords splendid views of nearby Canouan Island.

Constructed by Arne Hasslequist to specifications prepared by Oliver Messel, Casa Dalla Valle was built to the requirements of Gustave Dalla Valle, who has since sold the property and is now a prominent member of California's Napa Valley wine community.

Under its new owner, a number of improvements have been made, all faithful to Messel's grand design, which envisioned a group of elegant miniature villas surrounding the main building. Approached by an elliptical stone driveway, the main villa is built around an open courtyard and fountain with steps leading down to the expansive main living room. With its open construction, light fabric-covered furniture, mosaic stone tables, and cool blue-gray flooring, the room seems to float among the towering ferns that surround it.

There is a noticeable and welcome absence of rattan in Casa Dalla Valle's decor, which is clearly designed for comfort. The

Casa Dalla Valle's open courtyard.

The living room (right) is surrounded by a number of patios and walkways (above) offering spectacular views of the neighboring islands.

house's feeling of unaffected naturalness is accented by the presence of many items drawn from the island's environment. Nuggets of white coral in various sizes and gleaming black tortoise shells adorn the living room and its king-size coffee table. The salmon-colored walls are decorated with primitive art and a high, rough-beam ceiling supports a large chandelier and two huge fans. Large double doors lead out to patios and beautifully landscaped walkways. There are few confining walls; almost every direction provides a clear, sweeping view of the island and the sea.

Similarly, the dining gazebo with its wood and leather furnishings and fan palms presents spectacular views of the neighboring islands. The peach-and-gray suite in one of the outer buildings features four white louvered doors that fold back onto a balcony overlooking the sea.

Casa Dalla Valle is a house that invites its guests to linger and explore its many delightful features. Its plentiful open space is also conducive to entertaining, with ample room for guests to enjoy festivities throughout the house.

Far left: *This charming, vine-covered, walkway is a delightful example of Oliver Messel's design, marrying Mediterranean ambience with tropical colors.* Left: *The outdoor dining gazebo.* Next page: *Another view of the main villa's step-down living room.*

PARTICULARS

Details:
Six bedrooms
Accommodates twelve
Full staff includes butler,
cook, maid, two gardeners
Two dining pavilions
Use of jeep and pickup
truck

Contact:
The Mustique Co. Ltd.
P.O. Box 349
St. Vincent and the Grena-
dines
West Indies

Telephone:
(809) 458-4621/4653

Left: *The formal dining area
glows in the gathering dusk,
with the verdant shoreline of
Mustique islet framed by the
open sliding doors.*

Fili tou Anemou

The Cyclades have been known to seafarers and adventurers for almost six thousand years. For visitors today as for those early travelers, they seem cast down from Mount Olympus by the ancient gods of Greece, who must have thought the crystalline waters of the Aegean Sea to be the perfect setting for these gemlike islands.

Today the gods may well envy the mortals who have made these myth-surrounded, sun-drenched islands a haven from the frenetic pace of the twentieth century. Here is the oasis of tranquility immortalized by the poetry of John Masefield, who described the Cyclades as "cloaked in a purple mystery . . . where dolphins perform offshore in the sheer joy of life."

At the center of this peaceful realm is enchanting Síros, the capital island, with its sand beaches and lacey coasts. Here on a promontory overlooking the sea is a gleaming white-terraced villa named Fili tou Anemou ("Friends of the Wind"), the winter residence of Sir Richard and Lady Musgrave. The setting is beguiling, offering extraordinary vistas of the Aegean.

The white walls of the villa are set off by beamed ceilings, tiled floors, stone terraces, and colorful furnishings designed to harmonize with the surroundings. Sun worshipers will appreciate the sun terrace carved into the villa's rocky perch with steps leading down to deep-water swimming at sea level. Beaches are within walking distance.

Each of five spacious bedrooms has its own connecting private bath, and there is a small children's dormitory with bunk beds. A sitting room and a fully equipped modern kitchen round out the accommodations.

Previous page and above: *Winding steps from a swimming grotto lead up to the villa. Its rocky promontory overlooks the Aegean Sea and surrounding islands. Left: Fili tou Anemou's gleaming white terrace offers a panoramic view and an ideal setting for outdoor luncheons.*

Guests can bring a car onto the island for transportation and exploration, using the daily car ferry from Rafina on the Greek mainland. A waterskiing boat and two windsurfers are provided as well as two cars (local law permits only the staff to drive these).

Four and a half hours' sailing time from Rafina or Piraeus, Síros offers visitors considerable sports opportunities and entertainment diversions. A Greek Kahiki boat that sleeps eight is available for hire and is an ideal vessel for traveling to any of the neighboring islands.

Ermoúpolis, the chief town on Síros, has an archaeological museum featuring Cycladic art from the Bronze Age. Kini, on the western coast, is a quaint fishermen's village with sand beaches, an inn, and seaside restaurant. At Aghia Varvara, the site of an Orthodox Greek monastery, handmade textiles and embroideries can be purchased.

Other island facilities include three cinemas, tennis, friendly *tavernas,* rowing, sailing, fishing, and skin diving. Hunters will enjoy game shooting featuring dove, quail, and an unusual island feature: turtle.

PARTICULARS

Details:
Five bedrooms
Five bathrooms
Children and pets permitted
A staff of three including a cook and maid service
A staff-run motorboat included with house rental
Contact:
At Home Abroad, Inc.
Sutton Town House
405 East 56th St., 6H
New York, NY 10022
Att.: Claire Packman or Barry Shepard

Telephone:
(212) 421-9165

Previous page: *The winter residence of Sir Richard and Lady Musgrave, Fili tou Anemou is resplendent at sunset.* Left: *With white walls offset by beamed ceilings and tile floors, Fili tou Anemou is furnished in harmony with its surroundings.*

Laucala Island

Publisher Malcolm Forbes, a highly successful entrepreneur and multimillionaire, has taken the Walter Mitty fantasy world that dwells in the meekest of us and recreated it on his lush "island in the sun," Laucala.

A paradise in the Yasawa-Fiji group, just off the international date line, Laucala is one of the first islands to catch the rays of the rising sun and greet the new day. Here Forbes's thriving coconut plantation and luxury vacation resort are maintained by native residents. Expect a hearty "Bula" ("Welcome") when Forbes' twin-engine executive Piper Chieftain, the *Capitalist Tool Too,* sets down at Laucala's "international aerodrome." As Captain Bligh discovered when he made course for Laucala as a refuge after the Bounty mutineers set him adrift in an open boat, the island's population is friendly, generous, and enthusiastic.

Laucala was until recently the least known of the remote Fijis, and indeed the limited guest accommodations Forbes has provided have helped to keep it that way. The feeling of informal ease and privacy here is unduplicated at any of the so-called luxury resorts in the world. This is truly an aquatic sports Eden where one tests one's skills against the challenge of black Pacific sailfish, marlin, yellowfin tuna, sharks, and barracuda.

True fishermen can be secure in the knowledge that few lines have been cast in these virtually virgin waters. The turquoise-cobalt, vividly transparent sea hides flowered coral reefs that teem with caches of rare tropical fish. It is a treasure trove for scuba diving and snorkeling, a magnificent environment where one can take striking photographs of Neptune's underworld.

Guests are housed in *bures,* or cottages, modern duplications of the traditional native huts with handcrafted woven walls and cathedral thatched roofs. Each cottage nestles beneath the towering

A paradise in the Yasawa-Fiji group, Laucala is one of the first islands to catch the rays of the rising sun.

97

palms whose fanning effect is stirred by the prevailing trade winds. Should one desire, the mechanical air-conditioning system of the cottage can be switched off in favor of the naturally cooling breeze and the murmur of the palms.

The cottages are self-contained units with fully equipped kitchens, stocked pantries, and modern shower-baths. No detail of comfort or luxury has been overlooked, from the complimentary bar to the bowls of fresh fruit and flowers.

Guests feast on gala meals for which the ingredients are gathered locally from sea and tree or from the farm on the estate (which stocks its own chickens and has a bountiful vegetable garden). Dinners are served at the main Plantation House, but breakfast is prepared by a cook or housekeeper in the privacy of one's cottage. A stay at Laucala reveals a part of the world once known only to such great writers as Maugham and Michener.

PARTICULARS

Details:
Four air conditioned guest houses accommodating up to eight people
Glass-bottomed boat
Swimming pool
Tennis
Deep-sea fishing boat
Fishing gear and tackle
Scuba equipment
Waterskiing
Wind surfing

Contact:
Fiji Manager
Attn. Errol Ryland
Ft. Garland, Co. 81133

Telephone:
(719) 379-3263

Telex:
4976112 FT

Far left and left: *Two views of the main plantation house where the guests are served dinner.*

Sundial

Somehow Columbus managed to miss Barbados during his many voyages, so settlement of this West Indian gem was left to the British, who grafted their common laws and ancient traditions onto the African heritage of the native inhabitants. Today, this twenty-mile-long island—which became independent in 1966—has become the site of some of the loveliest vacation homes in the Western hemisphere. On its southwestern shore, in exclusive Saint James Parish, is Sundial House, originally designed and built by the late Miles Gray of Santa Barbara.

Gray, who deeply admired the Palladian school of architecture, created a design for Sundial that gives the residence the character and appearance of an old French country chateau. This impression is heightened by the exterior pillars and white louvered shutters. Entering the spacious, high-ceilinged, living room from the outer portico, one feels suspended in time.

Of the two bedroom suites, one has a magnificent armoire in addition to an exquisitely beautiful chest. In the master bedroom, twin beds are joined by an immense headboard with a fabric covering that extends up the wall, creating a canopy effect. The walls are of coral stone, a material used throughout the house.

Windows in both bedrooms are constructed with louvered shutters that open out on the patios and terraces. The master bedroom has a skirted table and an antique armoire and secretary. The two bedrooms are connected by a secret passageway.

Sundial's patios and terraced grounds were designed to lure guests outdoors. The expansive rear patio, with its two balustrades and pineapple statuary, is reached through the living room's fourteen-foot wooden doors. A pillared breakfast terrace just off the kitchen overlooks the landscaped yard, the setting for a lily pond that is set off by the surrounding statues and fountain.

The living room's fourteen-ft. wooden doors lead out to the rear patio.

101

Barbados still reflects a colorful cross-section of its two heritages. The snappy harbor police go about their daily business in uniforms styled after those of the British seamen of Lord Nelson's day. Young boys still dive for coins thrown from the cruise ships anchored in port, and gaily costumed peddlers called "higglers" hawk their wares in the marketplace. For special holiday celebrations the Regimental Fife and Drum Corps turns out in red, gold, and blue, while the mounted police cut a fancy turn in their leopard-skin tunics.

PARTICULARS

Details:
Two master suites with private bathrooms
Guests' use of a nearby private beach
Golf privileges at a nearby course
Tennis privileges at a nearby court
Maid and butler/chef

Contact:
Caribbean Home Rentals, Inc.
Att.: Timothy H. Roney
Post Office Box 710
Palm Beach, FL 33480

Telephone:
(409) 833-4454

Cable:
AJOUPA

Far left: *Sundial's living and dining rooms.* Left: *The patios and terraced grounds are ideal for enjoying meals and afternoon tea.*

North Dumpling Island

A faint glow slowly rises from the waters of the sound, dismissing the darkness from Moon Watching Mountain, a man-made knoll on the southeastern rim of North Dumpling Island. Soon the orange glow obliterates the sentinel beam of the lighthouse lamp. Daybreak has come to this private two-acre retreat just off the Connecticut coast.

The island and its vigilant lamp have greeted the dawn in this manner for almost 150 years. Yet its history actually extends back to precolonial days, when it was discovered by Captain Adrian Block, who first navigated the waters of Long Island Sound in 1609. Inspired by the extreme height of this small spit of land floating dumpling-like on the sea, Block named it and built the island's first structure, claiming it for King James II.

Today, only five owners (but numerous costly modern additions) later, that same building—known as the Lighthouse—is a delightful three-bedroom residence with its own electrical generating and water purification systems. North Dumpling offers the privacy of island living along with easy access to the major metropolitan centers of the northeast corridor between New York City and Boston. (For example, the island is a short boat ride away from Mystic and a two-minute helicopter flight from the Groton–New London airport.)

Groves of Japanese black pines, weeping willows, mountain laurels, and fruit trees surround the base of the main house. A path lined with tulips and the fragrant blossoms of bayberry, azaleas, and daffodils leads up to an intricately hand-carved front door. Inside, the decor is comfortably modern with a decided nautical

On a foggy night one can imagine a captain's wife standing watch on the traditional widow's walk, as the lighthouse and its tolling bell alert passing mariners to the rocky shoals below.

*Local clammers and lobster-
men bring succulent seafood to
the island's dock.*

theme. In the richly paneled study just off the main foyer, the shelves exhibit fine examples of scrimshaw, the whaler's art of ivory carving. The carved fireplace is set off by blue and white tiles embellished with sailing ships.

A spacious, glass-walled living room finished in white, with a salmon and white marble fireplace, offers a different mood. A promenade deck runs around the main level. One flight below a cherry-paneled taproom is furnished with two dining tables and an antique Brunswick pool table.

The adjoining wine cellar, open to guests, is said to be the domain of three friendly ghosts who look after the island and its visitors. Believed to be the spectral remains of Captain Block's son, a lighthouse keeper, and a sea captain, they are reputed to share a deep appreciation of the grape. A bottle of Beaujolais and one of Riesling are kept open for their nocturnal imbibing.

The formal dining room is the showcase for a series of paintings by Eveline Roberge depicting the harbors of Mystic and Boston when seafaring was the way of life in New England.

Clammers and lobster men still farm the waters of the sound, and visitors can step into the past in the carefully restored village of Old Mystic. New England's reputation for fine dining can be verified by a visit to any of the highly rated restaurants in the area, or guests can enjoy a fresh lobster catch collected from the sea by North Dumpling's resident caretaker.

As the day ends, climb the stairs to the lighthouse as its light turns on and the beacon cuts through the gathering dusk. Settle in the snug "poet's corner" or the circular widow's walk, and watch the sun return to the sea framed through the Temple of the Four Winds, a re-creation of Stonehenge built on the western edge of the island.

North Dumpling's inviting study, with its detailed fireplace, features intriguing examples of scrimshaw, the whalers' art of whalebone carving.

PARTICULARS

Details:
Three bedrooms
Two whirlpools and
steambaths
Accommodates ten
Five boats
Helicopter pad
Full-time caretaker
Cook/Maid available

Contact:
Mr. Dean Kamen
340 Commercial Street
Manchester, NH 03101

Telephone:
(603) 669-5139

Previous page: *Sliding glass
doors on both sides of the spacious living room open to the
promenade deck that encom-
passes the main level. A marble fireplace offers a different
mood in the evening when the
sun's rays slip over the mainland.* Left: *The snug tap
room, with an antique Brunswick pool table, is ready for
an evening's competition after
a day on North Dumpling.*

San Michele

*F*rom the earliest days of the Union Jack, the British have sought out the world's loveliest islands. Washed by blue waters, cooled by tropical breezes, these remote paradises served as colonial outposts and vacation retreats. Jamaica in particular proved an irresistible magnet for royalty and commoner alike. With the pearl-and-emerald setting of its white beaches and lofty green mountains, the island became a haven far from the harsh uncertainties of the British climate, and was at one time considered the British capital in the Caribbean.

Tucked away on the southwesternmost tip of the island is Bluefields Bay, a region whose history traces back to Spanish rule and the establishment of a small group of European refugees in the early 1500s. Their small colony-settlement created a gracious way of life that still exists at San Michele, a tranquil beach residence just twenty-five feet from the water's edge. Few visitors to Jamaica know of its existence, and fewer still have experienced the pleasures afforded by its seclusion.

San Michele's guests are transported back to earlier days the moment they land at Montego Bay's airport for the chauffeured drive to the residence. On an acre of grounds surrounded by the bay on three sides, San Michele is a long way from the pressures of twentieth-century life. Stands of bamboo, mango trees, dugout canoes, unspoiled reefs, and an equally unspoiled bordering village vie for the attention. Here the selection of activities ranges from snorkeling, fishing, boating, and windsurfing to tennis and croquet or simply relaxing in a hammock with a good book and a cool drink.

San Michele itself is actually composed of a compound of three structures. The main building has a large, comfortably furnished living room that extends almost the length of the house. Its doors and windows frame the sea at the back of the house much

Sharing the same coastline as the resort of Negril, San Michele's sense of privacy is protected by mango trees and stands of bamboo.

as the porticos of the veranda frame the front vista. Two queen-size bedrooms and baths, a dining veranda, and a kitchen complete the dwelling. Steps away to the rear are two outer buildings. One, for additional guests, contains a bedroom with a king-size four-poster, another room with twin beds, and two bathrooms. A smaller building houses the staff.

A wooden footbridge stretches out to a nearby small offshore islet with its own gazebo. Here is an ideal location from which to marvel at the legendary tropical sunsets as they turn the sea from orange-copper to a deep mauve.

PARTICULARS

Details:
Capacity for eight guests
Four bedrooms
Private pool
Twenty-four-hour tennis
Fully staffed

Contact:
International Advisory
Group, Inc.
Att.: Mr. and Mrs.
C. Braxton Moncure
726 North Washington St.
Alexandria, VA 22314

Telephone:
(202) 232-4010

Far left: *Chilled champagne is an accompaniment to the setting sun that slips below the horizon, turning the sea's colors from orange-copper to a deep mauve.* Left: *A wooden footbridge stretches out to a small offshore islet with its own gazebo.*

Milestone Cottage

When Herbert Hart, Jamaica's banana king, built Milestone Cottage to be his personal summer hideaway, little did he realize that he was creating one of the world's most alluring "escape" cottages. He wanted a private retreat that would take full advantage of the island's great natural beauty, a home that would reflect his love for Jamaica by blending totally with its environment.

Hart's unique design, by setting Milestone almost on the edge of a hidden cove on Bluefields Bay, affords full exposure to the splendor of the bay and the surrounding gardens and natural foliage. The house's singular feature, a fold-away accordion-type livingroom wall, allows the staff to modify this exposure to suit the changing moods of visitors or the elements.

Named after the historic milestones that once measured off distances from Spanish Town, the island's former capital, the cottage displays at its front gate an actual milestone, a carefully preserved marker that bears the figure "107."

Along with the residence San Michele, Milestone was once part of a vast plantation. The property was sold off in parcels during the years before and after World War II, but San Michele and Milestone have now been united once again through the efforts of the current proprietors, Mr. and Mrs. C. Braxton Moncure.

Bluefields Bay, on the southwestern tip of the island far from the more populated areas to the north and east, played an important part in Jamaica's colorful history. In the 1500s, when the Spanish ruled the "main," its waters were known as the Bay of Oristano. Its deep, reef-protected harbor and important fresh-water access made it one of the prime settlement areas on the island.

Previous page: On the edge of a hidden cove, Milestone, named after the stones that once measured off distances from Spanish Town, has a commanding view of Blue-fields Bay. Below: *Luxury reaches its zenith when guests awake to savor the aroma of freshly brewed Jamaican coffee—served in bed on gleaming silver with a cornucopia of local fruits.*

No less an illustrious figure than the noted Welsh buccaneer Sir Henry Morgan was responsible for renaming the bay "Blew-fields." When the English captured Jamaica in 1655 and designated the pirate the first general of the new colony, he promptly made the bay an anchorage for his fleet of privateers. From this picturesque site, where whales came to birth their calves, Morgan launched his forays against other Spanish holdings in the Caribbean. It was from here that he set sail for the sacking of Panama.

Today, for guests dining at Milestone Cottage, the serenity of the bay belies its swashbuckling history. The living and dining areas of the cottage are flanked by patios that open onto the pool and spa. Antique Spanish water vessels decorate the pool and the steps leading to the seaside patio.

To the rear of the house is the spacious master bedroom with

The living and dining areas of the cottage are flanked by patios that open onto the pool and spa.

its Italian marble floors, traditional mahogany four-poster bed, and private bath. The lace-curtained windows look out on the sparkling Caribbean waters. Handcrafted mahogany furniture is featured throughout the cottage.

All meals at Milestone are carefully prepared by a gourmet, French-trained native cook. Menus utilize the full range of fresh Jamaican food, including lobsters and fish that are brought to the cottage daily by natives in dugout canoes and fruits and vegetables grown directly on the property.

PARTICULARS

Details:
Accommodates three
Private pool
Whirlpool bath
Full staff

Contact:
International Advisory
Group, Inc.
Att.: Mr. and Mrs.
C. Braxton Moncure
726 North Washington St.
Alexandria, VA 22314

Telephone:
(202) 232-4010

Antique Spanish water vessels decorate the patio and pool that overlook the white sand beach and the waters of Bluefields Bay.

Mele Komo

Dramatic, rugged headlands and deep, wild gorges that crash hundreds of feet into the Pacific mark the coast of Maui, the second largest land mass in the volcanic Hawaiian chain. It is an island of hidden coves and snug bays interspersed with fine sandy beaches.

Ever since its siren call first beckoned early Polynesian settlers from across the broad sea, Maui's song of greeting, "E kome mai"—"Come inside"—has provided a warm welcome to all who visit her friendly shores. Many visitors stay to relax under the tradewinds that caress the magical slopes of Mount Haleakala, one of the world's largest volcanic craters, before moving on to bustling Oahu, or Hawaii, better known as the "Big Island."

On the lower slopes of Haleakala, a dream residence named Mele Komo extends its own warm welcome to "come inside" and stay a while. Built on the sixteenth fairway of the championship Wailea Golf Course, Mele Komo is about a mile from the beach. Yet its elevation offers broad views of the Pacific with aquatic ballets of whales against a backdrop of offshore islands and dramatic sunsets.

The moment one comes up the drive and enters the grounds of Mele Komo it is easy to understand why the house's distinctive juxtaposition of geometric forms earned it Wailea's Best Architectural Design Award. Unusual angles, gracefully rounded columns, and cubes of various sizes partition the open spaces of the two-and-a-half-story structure.

The upper level contains three bedrooms, each with a private bath, and there is an additional guest powder room. On the lower level are the living and dining rooms. The outer deck features a pool, spa, and barbecue facilities for alfresco dining.

The wonders of Maui invite constant exploration. Molokini, one of five offshore islands, is actually a volcanic crater whose lip extends above the water line. Beneath its waters are colorful trop-

Previous page: *Previous page: Mele Komo at sunset. Left: Built on the lower slopes of Haleakala, Mele Komo's open design allows the night trade winds to cool the dining room. Above: One of Mele Komo's three amply sized bedrooms.*

ical coral and volcanic reefs, the home of countless brightly tinted schools of fish. The island is a marine sanctuary that is eagerly sought out by scuba divers and snorkelers. Excursions can be arranged to Molokini, as well as to the other outlying islands.

The major attraction on Maui is, of course, Mount Haleakala, towering a majestic 10,023 feet into the sky. Hardy visitors gather here each dawn to watch the rising sun apparently emerge from its nightly slumber in the dormant crater. Astronauts train on Haleakala's desolate slopes because its barren terrain so closely resembles the moon's surface.

A winding highway leads to Hana, site of the famous seven pools formed by waterfalls cascading down from Haleakala's heights. Legend says that Hawaii's ancient kings bathed in these sacred waters. Not far from Hana is Kipahulu, the final resting place of explorer-aviator Charles A. Lindbergh.

PARTICULARS

Details:
Three bedrooms, three bathrooms
Spa, pool
Golf
Boat and car included
Working office

Contact:
Villas of Hawaii
4218 Waialae Ave.,
Suite 203
Honolulu, Hawaii 96816

Telephone:
(800) 522-3030

Mele Komo's distinctive juxtaposition of geometric forms earned it Wailea's Best Architectural Design Award.

Hope Island

*W*hen Lillian Gish, Bette Davis, Vincent Price, and the supporting cast of *The Whales of August* used Hope Island as their on-location residence while filming that critically acclaimed motion picture, they became the latest visitors to discover the allure of this eighty-five-acre storybook retreat.

Hope Island is situated in Casco Bay, an unspoiled setting five miles off the coast of Maine. Close enough to the mainland for easy access, yet remote enough to be free of land-bound instrusions, this tranquil paradise first served as a haven and hunting ground in the seventeenth century for the local Indians who sought relief from mainland summer temperatures.

In the 1920s, wealthy East Coast families established the island as a summer refuge. The care that went into developing such residences as Hope Island's lodge is obvious today, after four generations of family ownership.

Romantically set on a slope with an expansive view of the sea, the house is a solid New England fortress of privacy. Behind its shuttered Yankee facade is a world of crackling fireplaces, generous accommodations, and luxuriously comfortable furnishings. Bedrooms appointed with brass and iron beds line sunlit corridors. The Great Room with its library, piano, and majestic stone fireplace provides a center for the indoor activities that often spill over to the adjacent parlor lounge.

Outside, the Atlantic provides an aquatic stage for dolphin and sea lion viewing and bird watching. Fishing is ideal, with schools of tuna, blues, and swordfish abounding in the deep waters nearby. Lobsters to highlight an evening's clambake are delivered each morning to the island's dock by local fishermen.

Everywhere the natural setting of the island has been consciously preserved, from the sweeping bay and the many private coves to the interior walking trails bordered by towering pines and open, flowering meadows. Here is an ideal retreat for writers, philosophers, and quiet souls.

PARTICULARS

Details:
Thirteen-bedroom lodge
Five bathrooms
Accommodates twenty
guests
Staff of seven in attendance
Three full-menu meals
served daily
Facilities for all water
sports
Tennis, golf, and night life
within boating distance

Contact:
John B. Harlow II
Hope Island Club
P.O. Box 254
Locust Valley, NY 11560

Telephone:
(212) 877-8294

Previous page: *This private,
85-acre island abounds with
towering pines, rose-lined
paths, slopes of bayberry, and
promises of complete solitude.*
Right: *The interior shows a
studied simplicity with an
abundance of charm and
grace.*

Haleakala

Rising from the lush tropical growth of Oahu, to tower above the swaying palms is Haleakala, a guest residence named after the crater of Maui Island. At first glance the modern-day counterpart of an ancient Polynesian tiki, this architectural treasure is set against the cliffs of Diamond Head, seemingly cleaved from the rocks of that natural wonder.

One of Hawaii's most celebrated residences, it is a completely modern structure that combines "tree house" ambience with state-of-the-art technology. At night its striking facade resembles a towering space vehicle about to leap into the star-sprinkled sky.

Haleakala's spacious living areas greet the sun from every angle to capture every dramatic element of Hawaii's natural splendor and climate. The residence is crowned by a stunning luxury dome that is ideal for candlelight dining beneath the canopy of the South Cross.

One of the features of this remarkably designed estate is the elevator that leads to aerielike living quarters. Large bedrooms, each with its own private bath, share the first residential level with a spacious study and library. A fully equipped Jacuzzi is glass enclosed, surrounded by a glade-like setting crowned by Diamond Head itself.

Three tiled decks are the main feature of the top level, each with a dazzling view of the Pacific. Within is the plush living room with its custom-built audio-visual center and a movable sky curtain to control the light and shade entering through the domed skylight.

The top level also contains a completely equipped kitchen. Throughout the interior rooms and adorning the outer decks is a colorful profusion of tropical plants, an extension of the island paradise that surrounds Haleakala on all sides.

Haleakala rises from lush tropical growth; a modern counterpart of an ancient Polynesian Tiki.

133

The residence offers the exclusive privacy of a mountain retreat, yet Haleakala is only moments away from the luxuriant beaches of Waikiki, just one of the natural attractions of this Eden-like land.

The island's population reflects its multiethnic heritage as crossroads of the Pacific. The same diverse influences—including Japanese, Chinese, and Filipino elements—are found in its culture, food, and entertainment. Waikiki, which lies between Haleakala and the capital city of Honolulu, boasts broad beaches with surfboarding and outrigger canoe races by day and a pulsating night life with world-class dining.

Above: *A luxurious outdoor hot tub allows guests to bask in the "tree house" ambience of Haleakala, with dazzling views of the Pacific from a tri-patio top level.*

Right: *A wide-angle view graphically details the major elements of Haleakala's remarkable beauty. All-exposure sun decks surround the comfortably designed upper living room.*

Famed for its cane sugar and pineapples, Hawaii has many other food specialties, including poi (a paste made from taro root), coconut, passion fruit, guava, papaya, Macadamia nuts, and roast pig—all of which can be sampled at an easily arranged luau feast.

Although it is only the third largest of the islands in the Hawaiian group, Oahu's varied features make it the hub of visitor activity. Historians will appreciate the museums and World War II monuments. Sports lovers will relish the yachting, deep-sea fishing, water sports, hang gliding, and horseback riding.

For those who simply want to explore on their own, a highway circles the island with connecting roads that link the rugged coast with fertile inner valleys, forests, and the famed extinct volcanos of Koko Head and the Punchbowl as well as Haleakala's neighbor, Diamond Head.

PARTICULARS

Details:
Four bedrooms
Five bathrooms
Two jacuzzis (one in master bedroom)
Maids' quarters
5 stories with elevator
and staircase
Contact:
Pacific Island Adventures
4218 Waialae Ave., Suite
203-A
Honolulu, Hawaii 96816

Telephone:
(808) 735-9000
(800) 522-3030

Previous page: *One of three residential levels, the living room has a custom-built audio-visual center and movable sky curtain.* Far left: *At night, architectural lighting paints and highlights Haleakala's dramatic facade, conjuring the image of a space vehicle about to leap into a starry sky.* Left: *The crowning luxury dome, ideal for candlelight dining beneath the canopy of the South Cross.*

Castles and Courts

Mallow Castle

No part of Ireland more clearly deserves the appellation "Emerald Isle" than the county of Cork. Nowhere else in this enchanted land are the mountains greener or the lakes bluer. Rocky headlands along the coast tame the fierce Atlantic gales, allowing the temperate Gulf Stream to nourish a blanket of flower-bedecked valleys. Here in the southwestern part of the Republic of Ireland, north of the town of Cork and east of Killarney, lies the town of Mallow. Here, where myth, history, nature, and a "bit of the Blarney" fuse, creating the Ireland of whimsy and legend, is Mallow Castle.

In a land literally teeming with great castles, Mallow is almost an anachronism. Its low silhouette resembles a comfortable English country manor house more than it does a forbidding fortress. Yet this gray-white Elizabethan facade has witnessed more than its share of strife in Ireland's often turbulent history. In fact, the present structure, erected in the late 1600s, was created out of violence. The original Mallow Castle was set on fire by James II during the religious wars. Now the charred remains of the "old castle" stand opposite the "new castle," built after William of Orange defeated James at the famous battle of the Boyne.

Mallow's guests are graphically reminded of the sequence of events that form the history of Ireland, and the castle's participation, by the documents, books, and furnishings found throughout the house. All have been carefully conserved by the present owners, Judy and Michael McGinn, both Americans. Their search for a "wee 'umble cottage" in Ireland—to escape the semitropical summers of Washington, D.C., and to return to their ancestral roots—resulted in the purchase of Mallow in 1983. Fortunately for the guests who come to share this "manor-born" way of life, the McGinns have preserved and restored a nobleman's milieu.

143

Previous page: *Maintained for more than four centuries by the same family of Irish nobles, Mallow Castle now belongs to Michael and Judy McGinn.* Above: *The castle has a twenty-acre park with a herd of seventy white fallow deer—one of two such herds in the world.*

The distinctive twin towers of Mallow overlook the banks of the salmon-filled Blackwater River, which wends its way through Cork's charming countryside. A herd of rare white deer, a gift from Her Majesty Elizabeth II, frolic in a twenty-acre deer park that lies to the east. The deer's overgrown domain contrasts vividly with the broad green lawn bordering the terrace that stretches across the front of the residence.

The corner tower's immense portals lead into a massive entry hall. At the end of the hall is an artifact-filled drawing room with an intricately carved mantelpiece. Here too is the formal dining room, dominated by a portrait of William of Orange (a gift from the monarch to Sir William Jephson).

Until the McGinns purchased the castle, its ownership had rested with descendants of the Norreys-Jephson family for over four hundred years. Their portraits line the walls of the staircase

that lead to the inner court and to the second-floor bedrooms. Particularly magnificent is the tower bedroom's vista, which takes in the full sweep of the castle against a sunset framed by the ruins of the old castle.

In the dining room guests enjoy a Continental menu with occasional touches of traditional Irish fare, including fresh salmon and lamb from the estate's grounds accompanied by vegetables from the garden. Golf, tennis, fishing, and billiards are some of the diversions to be enjoyed on the estate.

Short excursions beyond Mallow's grounds include the Lakes of Killarney, the Rock of Cashel (where Saint Patrick preached), and Blarney Castle. Only twelve miles to the south, the adventurous can hang upside down, suspended eighty-five feet from the ground, to kiss the famous Blarney stone and receive the gift of everlasting eloquence.

Above: *The elm-paneled dining room is dominated by a larger-than-life-size portrait of William of Orange—a gift to Sir William Jephson from the Monarch himself.*

PARTICULARS

Details:
Eight bedrooms
Full staff of eight
One week minimum rental
period

Contact:
Michael McGinn
319 Maryland Ave., NE
Washington, DC 20002

Telephone:
(202) 547-7849

Right: *The intricately carved mantlepiece provides a dramatic focal point amidst the artifacts that fill Mallow Castle's drawing room.*

Hatton Castle

Scotland's place in British history and legend surely dwarfs its geographic stature. Its rugged coastline invited invasion from the marauding tribes of Picts, Celts, and Norsemen, yet the fierce northern waters of this "roof of the Empire" also provided a training ground for generations of British seamen and boat builders.

Deep in the eastern highlands, the two thousand-acre estate of Hatton Castle has marked the passage of history for over six hundred years. For almost half of that period—since 1709, when it was purchased by Alexander Duff—it has served as the ancestral home for twelve generations of Duffs.

Balquholly, the original estate house, was long ago incorporated into the structure of the present building. Following a renovation program in 1745, the house was renamed Hatton Lodge. Further alterations in the early 1800s resulted in another name change, and it has remained Hatton Castle ever since. Luxurious improvements have been added by the present laird and owner, David James-Duff of Hatton.

As befits a noble Scottish residence, Hatton is solidly built, with large, hospitable guest accommodations. The public rooms on the ground floor are exquisitely furnished; the well-tended grounds invite long strolls through the gardens and shrubberies and on to the splendid estate woodlands. A walled garden provides fresh produce for the castle's table, and the outer grounds teem with Scotland's wildlife. An excellent all-weather tennis court is situated close to the main building. Riding and pony trekking can be arranged, as well as visits to other historic houses, castles, and gardens. (Located 140 miles north of Edinburgh, close to Aberdeen, Hatton is in one of the loveliest parts of Scotland.) Excellent hunting and skeet shooting are available nearby, and trout and salmon abound in the estate's lochs and in the Don, Dee, Spey, and Deveron rivers.

149

Previous page: *Deep in the
eastern highlands, the two
thousand-acre estate of Hatton
Castle has marked the passage
of history for over six
hundred years.* Left: *Hatton
Castle is exquisitely furnished
with an eye for detail one is
likely to find only in a private residence.* Above: *With
gleaming silver and sparkling
crystal, the oval dining room
is set for an elegant dinner.
Experienced and innovative
cooks use the best of Scottish
beef, game, and fish as well
as vegetables from the Castle
garden. Fine wines from an
extensive cellar complement
the cuisine.*

Since golf is Scotland's national sport, visitors need not venture too far to find a challenging course. A pleasant eighteen-hole course can be visited in Turriff, a small market town only three miles away. Sturdier tests can be found at nearby Royal Aberdeen and Cruden Bay (about forty minutes by car) or at celebrated Saint Andrews and Gleneagles (a two hours' drive).

Tours can also be taken along the fabled Whisky Trail to visit the distilleries who produce Scotland's famous single malts. A "wee dram of the water of life," sipped before an open fire, is the perfect way to end a day at Hatton Castle.

Right: *One of Hatton Castle's eight bedrooms, with a four-poster bed, is a fine example of the sumptuous accommodations offered. The furnishings in this house were recently improved by the present owner, the twelfth Laird of Hatton.*

PARTICULARS

Details:
Eight bedrooms
Accommodates twelve
guests
Modern conveniences in-
cluding color TV,
billiards, table tennis, all-
weather tennis court

Contact:
Blandings
V. G. Williams Inc.
International Properties
2841 29th Street NW
Washington, D.C. 20008

Telephone:
(202) 328-1353

Chateau de Blanville

T ravel west by southwest, just past the outer ring of Parisian traffic. Suddenly the new industrial towns and modern suburban housing units fall away. Now tiny villages are sprinkled across the lush fields of wheat, corn, and mustard; narrow country lanes appear, bordered by an army of poplar trees marching their way through southern Normandy.

All at once, through the sunny haze, a small spire appears and begins to grow larger on the horizon. It is the Gothic silhouette of the cathedral of Chartres, set on a massive butte that completely dominates the surrounding landscape.

Only a few kilometers away from this historic structure is Chateau de Blanville, one of the most exquisite chateaux in France. Originally constructed in 1643, it changed hands at various times over the following century before coming into the possession of the descendants of Leonard du Cluzel, to remain in that family's hands for the next 250 years. The scion of an ancient Perigord family, du Cluzel extended the property considerably and installed formal French gardens inspired by the artistry of Le Norte who designed the gardens at Versailles.

Thérèse du Cluzel, Leonard's granddaughter, saved the estate from looting and possibly from ruin by remaining at the chateau throughout the revolutionary period. Her great-great-grandson, Count Charles-Louis Cosse Brissac, is the present owner. He and his wife still maintain a private apartment at the chateau in a secluded wing with their own entrance.

The chateau is protected by a grass moat, transversed by a vine-covered bridge to the inner court of honor. The front drive, entered through tall iron grill gates, passes the garden's formal

Previous page: *Originally constructed in 1643, Chateau de Blanville changed hands at various times over the following century before it was bought by Leonard du Cluzel of the Perigord family.*
Right: *The master suite's canopied bed is an example of the seventeenth-century furnishings faithfully restored by Blanville's present owner, Count Charles-Louis Cosse Brissac.*

hedges, ablaze in summer with the colors of geraniums and nasturtiums. The back drive extends over a half mile past the rear gardens, winding through the Blanville woods.

Blanville is in the heart of wild boar and stag country, and traditional hunting with hound packs can be arranged. The chateau stables also provide horses for countryside riding. A championship eighteen-hole golf course is about an hour's drive away, and guest membership can be arranged at a private club ten minutes from the residence. In season, fly fishing for trout and pheasant shoots can be scheduled.

PARTICULARS

Details:
Accommodates ten
Six bedrooms, all with
ornamental fireplaces with
working stoves
Five bathrooms
Heated pool
Fully staffed

Contact:
At Home Abroad, Inc.
Sutton Town House
405 East 56th Street
New York, NY 10022

Telephone:
(212) 421-9165

Previous page: *One of the main salons on Blanville's first level.* Right: *The estate's one thousand acres include working farms and woodlands. The formal gardens, still beautifully maintained, were inspired by the gardens of Versailles.*

Lismore Castle

*I*n the tranquil setting of Ireland's hills, in the beautiful Black-water Valley by the River Blackwater, stands Lismore Castle. Today no mounted horseman waits at the outer gatehouse to challenge visitors entering from the main road, yet the imagination readily conjures up a colorful past, for the castle's history is richly interwoven with many prominent names from Anglo-Irish history. Since the seventh century it has served as monastery, bishop's residence, knight's castle, and king's palace. Dukes and earls have claimed it as a manor house, and celebrities as varied as Sir Walter Raleigh and Adele Astaire have slept beneath its turrets.

No less than seven dukes of the Devonshire line have made their residence here since Lismore passed into the hands of the fourth duke in 1753 upon his marriage to Lady Charlotte Boyle, heiress to the earl of Cork. The original earl, Richard Boyle, dubbed the "Great Earl," purchased the Lismore property from the estate of Sir Walter Raleigh in 1602. Boyle arrived in Ireland in 1588 at the age of twenty-two, with a modest stake of twenty-seven pounds and the clothes on his back. He went on to amass enormous wealth in his lifetime, enlarging and embellishing the castle in the process.

Besides the residence bedrooms, guests are invited to use the grand yet comfortable public rooms—the drawing room, sitting room, dining room, billiards room, and banqueting hall. The highlight of every visit, however, is an exploration of Lismore Castle's magnificent grounds and gardens.

The lower garden, known as the Pleasure Grounds, is a spring garden, at its best in March and April, when it abounds in camellias, rhododendrons, and magnolias. A separate grove of camellias is planted at the bottom of the lower garden, with a vast bank of daffodils and narcissi under the east wing of the castle.

A long avenue flanked with stone walls leads to the upper

Previous page: *In the tranquil setting of Ireland's hills and the beautiful Blackwater Valley stands Lismore Castle.* Left: *The ceilings of the banquet hall were painted by Pugin, who designed much of the castle's furniture.* Right and next page: *The tapestries in the drawing room (to the right)* and in the sitting room (next page) *were designed by Tenier, depicting scenes from Don Quixote.*

gardens, built by the earl of Cork in 1626 and beautifully maintained by Lismore's present owner, Andrew Cavendish, the eleventh duke of Devonshire, who uses the castle as his Irish residence. Here the blossoms of the apple and pear orchard vie with a carpet of bulbs for the guest's attention. Yew hedges run behind the herbaceous borders of the Central Walk, which leads to the vegetable gardens of the top terrace. Two full-time gardeners attend the grounds, which comprise more than seven acres.

The castle grounds are also a sportsman's paradise, offering riding, hunting, and a challenging nine-hole private golf course.

The River Blackwater teems with salmon and trout, and the famous Careysville Salmon Fishery is part of the estate. Arrangements can also be made for deep-sea and big game fishing, as well as attendance at various horse races within a short distance from the castle.

Just a short walk away is the ancient town of Lismore. Waterford, the home of world-famous Waterford glass and crystal, is only forty-four miles to the north. Nearby Cork, on the River Lee, is a contrast of wide, bustling streets and narrow alleys in the older sections; the town offers excellent shopping and an opera house and theater.

PARTICULARS

Details:
Five double bedrooms
Four single bedrooms
Seven bathrooms
Maximum of twelve
guests accommodated
Fully staffed including but-
ler, cook, and resident
agent

Contact:
Paul Burton, Agent
Lismore Castle
County Waterford
Ireland

Telephone:
Dungarvan (058) 54424

Far left: *The dining room,
with its famous black marble
chimney piece originally ex-
hibited in 1851.* Left: *Family
portraits and tapestries decorate the halls of Lismore
Castle.*

Escape without Bounds

Never Say Never

*E*ven resting at dockside, awaiting the spark that will bring its powerful twin twelve-cylinder diesels roaring to life, the sleek, aerodynamically designed yacht *Never Say Never* promises romance and adventure on the high seas.

Custom-built by Oceanfast Shipyards (Perth, Australia) and owned by industrialist Gary Blonder, *Never Say Never* is one of the finest and fastest yachts ever created. The result of a remarkable team of artisans and nautical craftsmen, including Philip Curran Design, Australia's leading naval architects, and Jon Bannenberg, London's outstanding styling and interior design expert, the yacht is outfitted for maximum safety and capability.

No expense has been spared to provide a state-of-the-art electronic guidance system that places the world's oceans and seas within the yacht's cruising capability. Despite her commodious size—33.3 meters long with a beam of 6.98 meters—its 1.8 meter draft allows it to seek out secluded remote coves.

The captain, directing a crew of five, has complete control at all times, commanding the vessel's maximum speed of 34 knots from the wheelhouse, the satellite-linked main control center, or the flying bridge.

For the yacht's guests, every comfort has been provided. Dual master staterooms and guest staterooms are quipped with TVs and VCRs. Aft-deck floorboards can be raised for access to a large jacuzzi.

The careful design includes large closets, individual thermostats for the master air-conditioning system, writing desks, and bookshelves. The luxurious appointments of the staterooms in-

Left: *The luxurious master stateroom with queen-size bed.* Above: *The interior of* Never Say Never *with its contemporary elegance and fine leather furnishings.*

clude full-length mirrors and private baths, contemporary fur‐nishings in fine leather, and well-chosen artwork and sculpture. Little wonder that the *Never Say Never* has been a frequent nautical visitor on the popular NBC series "Miami Vice" and was featured in *Time* magazine.

PARTICULARS

Details:
Two Master staterooms
Two guest staterooms
Separate captain's cabin
and crew quarters
All necessary electronic
and navigational equipment

Contact:
Dynasty International
1323 S. E. 17th St., Suite
261
Ft. Lauderdale, FL 33316

Telephone:
(305) 522-4654

Telex:
153529 DYNASTY

The design of the dining salon typifies Bannenberg's use of spacious interiors.

Magic Lady

Combining speed and grace under sail, the yacht *Magic Lady* is aptly named. With her billowing, towering spinnaker catching the wind, she is a sorceress afloat who promises adventure and romance before the mast.

The 105-foot vessel is a rare marriage of speed and comfort, a unique combination among the world's first-class charter vessels. Designed and built for Charles Evans and S. A. ("Huey") Long by the world-renowned firm of John G. Alden, Inc., *Magic Lady* offers guests high racing performance and luxury accommodations.

The yacht is fully equipped with electrically powered Hood *Stoway* and Sea Fury systems. Should the wind die down, *Magic Lady* will cruise for two thousand miles at eleven knots. Yet because of its special acoustic systems the engine is barely audible. Under power, *Magic Lady* is as peaceful as under sail. The Navigation Station and Communication Center allows world-wide communications. The navigation and safety systems are all state-of-the-art.

The yacht's 17′ x 17′ main salon, the center of activities on board, includes a dining area that easily seats eight. On the starboard side are the ship's library and an entertainment center providing TV, stereo, and Betamax.

The on-deck dining area is ideal for balmy evenings under the stars. Appetites for gourmet meals prepared by the chef will be honed by a day of windsurfing, snorkeling, fishing, or waterskiing. And any tired muscles will soon be soothed in the separate fitness center's whirlpool bath and sauna.

The master stateroom, with its king-size bed, occupies the entire aft width of the vessel. There are enough hanging lockers and storage areas for long cruises. Two of the guest staterooms

Magic Lady's towering spinnaker billows in the wind, propelling her sleek form through the water. A sorceress afloat, she promises adventure and romance.

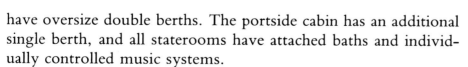

have oversize double berths. The portside cabin has an additional single berth, and all staterooms have attached baths and individually controlled music systems.

Magic Lady summers in the Mediterranean and winters in the Caribbean, ideal departure points for short excursions of a few days or lingering sea voyages of a month or more.

Statesman

*T*he elegance and style of the homes portrayed in these pages represent the *ne plus ultra* in luxury and comfort. As a fitting accompaniment, consider the Boeing 727, custom-designed jet *Statesman*: the ultimate in long-range personal transportation.

The moment you cross the threshold and are greeted by the steward, you enter a different realm. The *Statesman* is your personal magic carpet, poised to whisk you and your guests to any corner of the globe.

Inside, muted wood tones are tastefully accented by warm blue and off-white hues. The *Statesman* provides an excellent environment aloft for business or entertainment. The spacious interior design includes conversation areas, working spaces, and individual leather reclining loungers.

Service aboard the jet is impeccable in every way. The *Statesman*'s staff bring fine airborne dining to a superlative level. The Waterford crystal, bone china, and silver service are beautifully arrayed and the staff is ready to cater everything from hors d'oeuvres to dessert. Menus are prepared according to your specifications and the buffet and wet bar stocked to your preferences as specified prior to departure. Among the touches supplied for your in-flight diversion are two independent video tape systems for viewing first-run films, a library, a stereo music system, and a world-spanning electronic communication system.

The secluded private stateroom suite boasts a queen-size bed and an inviting lounge area. The adjoining dressing room and bath features gold fixtures, a marble vanity, and a hand-painted porcelain basin. A hot shower is available so that guests may arrive refreshed and relaxed at their destination.

Poised on the tarmac, ready for flight, the Statesman *and its crew are prepared to whisk you away to any destination in the world.*

183

The "up-front" features of the *Statesman* include some of the most advanced state-of-the-art technology ever incorporated on a commercial aircraft. With its three long-range navigation systems and auxiliary fuel system, the *Statesman*'s potential flight range is increased considerably. The powerful engines deliver greater cruising speeds, improved takeoff performance, and whisper-quiet operations. Here you will experience air travel as few ever encounter.

Left: *A hot shower, gold fixtures, marble vanity, and hand-painted porcelain basin are among the* Statesman's *luxury appointments. Above: Stretched out comfortably on the queen-size bed, you can enjoy a first-run film on one of the aircraft's two videotape systems.*

PARTICULARS

Details:
Maximum of twenty-four
passengers accomodated
Crew of six
Normal range 3,700 miles
Dash 9A Pratt & Whitney
jet engines
Auxiliary fuel system

Contact:
Mr. Jay Rifkin
Charters International
Group
17 Osgood Place
San Francisco CA 94133

Telephone:
415-398-2870

Telex:
910240 4958

*The warmth of flawlessly in-
laid hardwoods and leather
upholstery takes you beyond
conventional venues of flight.*

Grateful acknowledgment is due to the following photographers for their contribution to this project and for permission to reprint their photographs.

Nic Barlow, 40-47
Donna J. Callighan, 128-131
Nick Gleis, 182-187
Mark Green, 68-75
Michael Grimaldi, 12-23, 78-87,
    100-103, 170-175
Jack Kotz, 48-53
Rafaele Mascolo, 54-59
Charles Nes, 154-159
William Waterfall, 122-127,
    132-139

The photograph on pages 68-69 was provided by Jude Rilling of Dynasty International.

PUBLISHER'S NOTE

We wish to thank Robert Yerks of Mad River Design for his invaluable contribution to this project. We would also like to thank N.K. Graphics, Randi Jinkins, and Vince Beck for their design and production assistance. Lastly, we are grateful to Timothy Rooney of Caribbean Home Rental for his belief in this project.